Lots of Spots!

Written by Jane Clarke

Illustrated by Elisa Rocchi

Collins

Who and what is in this story?

Listen and say

Clare

spots

Jay

Teddy

dog

Doctor Clare was in her room. She had lots of things in her bag. She was ready to help.

Clare's brother Jay had a teddy bear.
Jay's teddy had lots of spots.

"Help! Teddy is ill," said Jay.

"Oh dear!" said Clare.

Jay wanted Doctor Clare to help his teddy.

"Let's see what's wrong," said Doctor Clare. She took out her thermometer.

Was Teddy hot last night?

Yes!

Doctor Clare looked in Teddy's eyes.
"He looks dizzy," she said.

Did he hit his head?

Yes!

Doctor Clare said, "That is not good."

"Is Teddy hungry?" asked Doctor Clare.
"No," said Jay.

That's not good.

Doctor Clare said, "Teddy is ill."

Doctor Clare got out her stethoscope.
She listened to Teddy's chest.

Doctor Clare said, "Teddy is very ill."

Doctor Clare looked at her computer.

Doctor Clare looked at Jay.

Teddy has teddy pox!

Is that bad?

Doctor Clare said, "Teddy pox is very bad."

"Teddy pox can make an ear drop off," said Doctor Clare. She got a bottle.

Doctor Clare got a bandage.

Doctor Clare looked at the dog. The dog had lots of spots, too. Doctor Clare looked at the dog's ear.

The dog has teddy pox, too!

15

Now, Jay had lots of spots!

"Is your ear falling off?"
asked Doctor Clare.

My ear?

"Don't worry, Jay," said Doctor Clare. "Doctors help people." Doctor Clare took off the red spots.

Doctor Clare gave Jay a big hug.
Doctor Clare had lots of spots, too.

Doctor Clare showed Jay the spots on the chair.

"Teddy pox is not real," said Doctor Clare.

It's only a game.

Phew!

Jay felt a lot better! And so did Teddy and the dog.

Picture dictionary

Listen and repeat

bandage

chest

dizzy

doctor

hug

medicine

spots

stethoscope

thermometer

1 Look and order the story

2 Listen and say

Collins

Published by Collins
An imprint of HarperCollins*Publishers*
Westerhill Road
Bishopbriggs
Glasgow
G64 2QT

HarperCollins*Publishers*
1st Floor, Watermarque Building
Ringsend Road
Dublin 4
Ireland

William Collins' dream of knowledge for all began with the publication of his first book in 1819.

A self-educated mill worker, he not only enriched millions of lives, but also founded a flourishing publishing house. Today, staying true to this spirit, Collins books are packed with inspiration, innovation and practical expertise. They place you at the centre of a world of possibility and give you exactly what you need to explore it.

© HarperCollins*Publishers* Limited 2020

10 9 8 7 6 5 4 3 2

ISBN 978-0-00-839689-3

Collins® and COBUILD® are registered trademarks of HarperCollins*Publishers* Limited

www.collins.co.uk/elt

British Library Cataloguing in Publication Data

A catalogue record for this publication is available from the British Library.

Author: Jane Clarke
Illustrator: Elisa Rocchi (Beehive)
Series editor: Rebecca Adlard
Commissioning editor: Zoë Clarke
Publishing manager: Lisa Todd
Product managers: Jennifer Hall and Caroline Green
In-house editor: Alma Puts Keren
Project manager: Emily Hooton
Editor: Frances Amrani
Proofreaders: Natalie Murray and Michael Lamb
Cover designer: Kevin Robbins
Typesetter: 2Hoots Publishing Services Ltd
Audio produced by id audio, London
Reading guide author: Emma Wilkinson
Production controller: Rachel Weaver
Printed and bound by: GPS Group, Slovenia

Download the audio for this book and a reading guide for parents and teachers at www.collins.co.uk/839689